IS IT TRUE GRANDFATHER?

♦ ♦ ♦

Wendy Lohse

Illustrated by

Jenny Sands

MACMILLAN
CARIBBEAN

'We're going to explore the mountain tomorrow, Grandfather,' said Flavien.

Grandfather Thomas gazed up at the mountain towering over the village and smiled. 'Oh, yes!' he said. 'We had such adventures up there when I was a boy. There are so many places to explore in the mountain.'

The old man's face – his eyes – his voice drew Flavien and Marie Claire closer. They knew when a story was forming behind the memory-filled eyes.

Flavien and Marie Claire crept closer to him. 'Tell us about an adventure, Grandfather,' said Flavien.

Auntie came out of the house and sat on the verandah chair opposite. Great Uncle Joseph strolled over, sat on the top step and leaned back against the verandah post, waiting for the old man's story to unfold.

'Eight, I was,' the old man began...

I was eight years old. Beth was five.
'You take care of Beth,' my mother said.
'She's never been exploring.'
Impatient to go, Beth dashed up the hill
to meet the others.

Joachim, the oldest, led the way, while Beth,
the youngest, struggled to keep up.

Up onto the mountain we scrambled, eating
the fruit and berries we picked as we walked.

Beth was feasting on hogplums
and we laughed at her purple face and hands.

'I'll carry you on my back, Beth,' said Joachim.
'I can walk,' she answered stubbornly.

Joachim led the others further up the mountain while I walked more slowly with Beth. They were a long way up ahead when they stopped.
Joachim called down to us,
'We're going into this cave, Thomas.'

Finally Beth and I reached the rocky
cave and I said, 'It's dark, Beth.
I'll hold your hand.'
'No!' she insisted. 'I can do it!'

The voices of the other children bounced
all around us as we walked a few steps
along the wide, rocky tunnel deeper into
the mountain. Gradually our eyes became
used to the darkness and thin shafts of light
pierced through the tiny crevices from the
world outside, casting strange shadows
all around.

Suddenly the tunnel branched away in two
directions. The others were calling,
'Thomas! Thomas! Thomas!
Hurry! Hurry! Hurry!', and the bouncing
voices confused Beth. But I was used to echoes.
'Down this way,' I said, racing ahead.

Soon the tunnel widened and I found the others sitting by
the edge of a small underground stream. I scooped some
water into my hands and drank thirstily.
'Where's Beth?' Joachim said.

I looked around. No Beth.
'Beth!' we called and our voices
bounced back at us.
'Beth! Beth! Beth!'
'Thomas? Thomas? Thomas?'
called Beth and her echoes.

'She might have gone into the other tunnel,' I said, and we all ran back to find her. Then we saw them. Not two, but three black arms of that tunnel stretching away into the mountain.

'Stay together,' Joachim ordered. We called out again and again, searching as far as we could go in every direction. But we heard no more from Beth.

The old man stopped his story and stared out towards the mountain. Many villagers sat around him. They were never too busy to listen to Grandfather Thomas's stories.

Whenever they heard the urgent whispered message, 'Grandfather Thomas is telling a story', they came.

Grandfather's eyes filled with tears which trickled freely down his face. 'We heard no more from Beth,' his voice trembled as he continued.

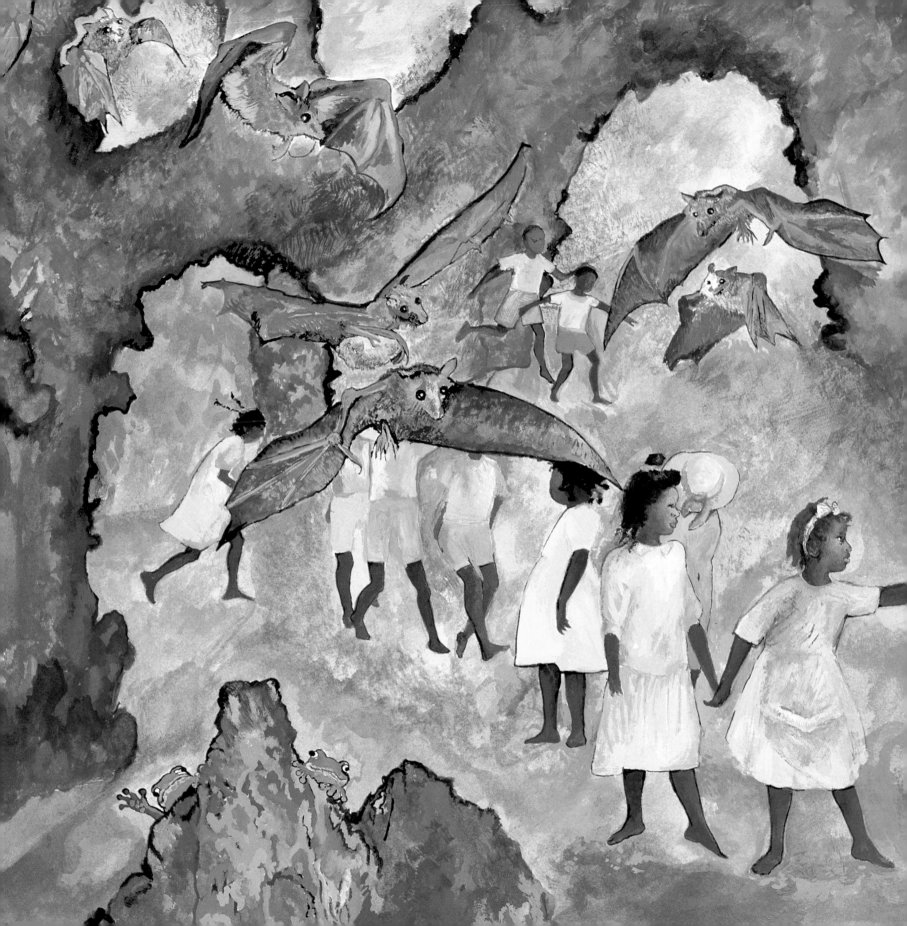

Beth was gone. There seemed to be so many narrow tunnels winding about within the mountain. Some tunnels branched off again and again. We were frightened for Beth – brave little Beth who pretended she was eight, not five.
'Take care of Beth,' my mother had said. And I had lost her.

By this time we were close to the mouth of the cave and could see that the sunlight outside had lost its brightness. We knew it was getting late. We would have to leave. Slowly, miserably we made our way out towards the mountainside.

We knew that within half an hour the sunset would be over and we'd be plunged into darkness.

'Don't worry,' said Joachim. 'We'll go to the village and get help. I'm sure we'll find her.'

I was scared. The tunnels would be even darker with no sun to shine through and I cried as I thought about leaving my little sister alone in that huge, dark mountain.

We clambered out into the fading sunlight crying, knowing that Beth would be frightened and alone.

Again the old man paused. Then as quickly as his tears began, his old eyes cleared and his nose crinkled.
'Just as we came out...' said Grandfather, his mouth creasing into a wide grin as he went on with the story.

Just as we came out from the cave we
heard a bright little voice accusing us.
'You took a long time!'
'Beth! Beth!' we all shouted at once, running
over to hug and touch her. Beth was
leaning against a tree eating hogplums again.

Joachim swung Beth around onto his back.
'You're riding home, Beth,' he said,
ignoring her loud protests.
'It's almost dark.'

Before long the darkness below was
speckled with dots of light bobbing up the
mountain. A search-party of villagers
had come to find us. Our father took
Beth from Joachim and hugged her.
'We couldn't find Beth,' Joachim explained.
'We thought she was lost.'

Beth was so tired she no longer protested
and allowed our father to carry her home.

Most of the village women, the little children
and the babies were here when we finally returned.
Beth's first exploring adventure had worried
them all.

'Where were you?' my mother asked anxiously.
'You've been away much too long!'

'Mmm,' murmured Beth. 'They all got lost.'

The old man leaned back in his chair and chuckled.

The village folk laughed too as they gathered their belongings and set off towards their homes. Laughter faded into the distance as the village and the mountain disappeared into the night.

'Is it true, Grandfather?' asked Marie Claire looking up at her Great-aunt Beth.

'It's true,' the old man smiled.

For Kathy. WL

For my sister, Helen and with special thanks to Donna. JS

Macmillan Education
Between Towns Road, Oxford OX4 3PP
A division of Macmillan Publishers Limited
Companies and representatives throughout the world

ISBN 0 333 66681 X

Copyright text © Wendy Lohse 1993
Illustrations © Jenny Sands 1993

First published 1993

First published by Scholastic Australia Pty Limited in 1993.
This edition published under licence from Scholastic
Australia Pty Limited

www.macmillan-caribbean.com

Printed and bound in Thailand

2008 2007 2006 2005
12 11 10 9 8 7 6 5 4